The Queen Bee & Other Nature Stories

Carl Ewald

The Queen Bee

THE farmer opened his hive. "Off with you!" he said to the bees. "The sun is shining, and everywhere the flowers are coming out, so that it is a joy to see them. Get to work, and gather a good lot of honey for me to sell to the shopkeeper in the autumn. 'Many a streamlet makes a river,' and you know these are bad times for farmers."

"What does that matter to us?" said the bees. But all the same they flew out; for they had been sitting all the winter in the hive, and they longed for a breath of fresh air.

They hummed and buzzed, they stretched their legs, they tried their wings. They swarmed out in all directions; they crawled up and down the hive; they flew off to the flowers and bushes, or wandered all round on the ground. There were hundreds and hundreds of them.

Last of all came the queen. She was bigger than the others, and it was she who ruled the hive.

"Stop your nonsense, little children," she said, "and set to work and do something. A good bee does not idle, but turns to with a will and makes good use of its time."

So she divided them into parties and set them to work.

"You over there, fly out and see if there is any honey in the flowers. The others can collect flower-dust, and when you come home give it in smartly to the old bees in the hive."

Away they flew at once. But all the very young ones stayed behind. They made the last party, for they had never been out with the others.

"What are we to do?" they asked.

"You! you must perspire," said the queen. "One, two, three! Then we can begin our work."

And they perspired as well as they had learned to, and the prettiest yellow wax came out of their bodies.

"Good!" said the queen. "Now we will begin to build."

The old bees took the wax, and began to build a number of little six-sided cells, all alike and close up to one another. All the time they were building, the others came flying in with flower-dust and honey, which they laid at the queen's feet.

"We can now knead the dough," she said. "But first put a little honey in—that makes it taste so much better."

They kneaded and kneaded, and before very long they had made some pretty little loaves of bee-bread, which they carried into the cells.

"Now let us go on with the building," commanded the queen bee, and they perspired wax and built for all they were worth.

"And now my work begins," said the queen, and she heaved a deep sigh; for her work was the hardest work of all.

She sat down in the middle of the hive and began to lay her eggs. She laid great heaps of them, and the bees were kept very busy running with the little eggs in their mouths and carrying them into the new cells. Each egg had a little cell to itself; and when they had all been put in their places, the queen gave orders to fix doors to all the cells and shut them fast.

"Good!" she said, when this was done. "I want you now to build me ten fine big rooms in the out-of-the-way parts of the hive."

The bees had them ready in no time, and then the queen laid ten pretty eggs, one in each of the big rooms, and the doors were fixed as before.

Every day the bees flew in and out, gathering great heaps of honey and flower-dust; but in the evening, when their work was done, they would open the doors just a crack and have a peep at the eggs.

"Take care," the queen said one day. "They are coming!"

And all the eggs burst at once, and in every cell lay a pretty little bee-baby.

"What funny creatures!" said the young bees. "They have no eyes, and where are their legs and wings?"

"They are grubs," said the queen. "You simpletons looked just like that yourselves once upon a time. One must be a grub before one can become a bee. Be quick now, and give them something to eat."

The bees bestirred themselves to feed the little ones, but they were not equally kind to them all. The ten, however, that lay in the large cells got as much to eat as ever they wanted, and every day a great quantity of honey was carried in to them.

"They are princesses," said the queen, "so you must treat them well. The others you can stint; they are only working people, and they must accustom themselves to be content with what they can get."

And every morning the poor little wretches got a little piece of bee-bread and nothing more, and with that they had to be satisfied, though they were ever so hungry.

In one of the little six-sided cells close by the princesses' chambers lay a little tiny grub. She was the youngest of them all, and only just come out of the egg. She could not see, but she could plainly hear the grown-up bees talking outside, and for a while she lay quite still and kept her thoughts to herself.

All at once she said out loud, "I could eat a little more," and she knocked at her door.

"You have had enough for to-day," answered the old bee who was appointed to be head bee-nurse, creeping up and down in the passage outside.

"Maybe, but I am hungry!" shouted the little grub. "I will go into one of the princesses' chambers; I have not room to stir here."

"Just listen to her!" said the old bee mockingly. "One would think by the demands she makes that she was a fine little princess. You are born to toil and drudge, my little friend. You are a mere working bee, and you will never be anything else all your days."

The Beehives

"But I want to be queen!" cried the grub, and thumped on the door.

Of course the old bee did not answer such nonsense, but went on to the others. From every side they were calling out for more food, and the little grub could hear it all.

"It is hard, though," she thought, "that we should have to be so hungry."

And then she knocked on the princess's wall and called to her, "Give me a little of your honey. Let me come into your chamber. I am lying here so hungry, and I am just as good as you."

"Are you? Just you wait till I am a reigning queen," said the princess. "You may be sure that when that time comes I shall not forget your impertinence."

But she had scarcely said this before the other princesses began to cry out in the most dreadful manner.

"You're not going to be queen! I shall be queen! I shall be queen!" they shrieked all together, and they began to knock on the walls and make a frightful disturbance.

The head bee-nurse came running up in an instant and opened the doors.

"What are your graces' orders?" she asked, dropping a curtsy and scraping the ground with her feet.

"More honey!" they shouted, all in one voice. "But me first—me first. I am the one who is to be queen."

"In a moment, in a moment, your graces," she answered, and ran off as fast as her six legs could carry her.

She soon came back with many other bees. They were dragging ever so much honey, which they crammed down the cross little princesses' throats. And then they got them to hold their tongues and lie still and rest.

But the little grub lay awake, thinking over what had happened. She longed so much for some honey that she began to shake the door again.

"Give me some honey! I can't stand it any longer. I am just as good as the others."

The old bee tried to hush her.

"Hold your tongue, little bawler! The queen's coming."

And at the same moment the queen bee came.

"Go your ways," she said to the bees; "I wish to be alone."

For a long time she stood in silence before the princesses' chambers.

"Now they are lying there asleep," she said at last. "From morning till evening they do nothing but eat and sleep, and they grow bigger and fatter every day. In a few days they will be full grown, and will creep out of their cells. Then my turn will be over. I know that too well. I have heard the bees saying to one another that they would like to have a younger and more beautiful queen, and they will chase me away in disgrace. But I will not submit to it. To-morrow I will kill them all; then I can remain queen till I die."

Then she went away. But the little grub had heard all she said.

"Dear me!" she thought; "it is really a pity about the little princesses. They are certainly very uppish, and they have not been nice to me, but still it would be sad if the wicked queen killed them. I think I will tell the old growler outside in the passage all about it."

She began once more knocking at the door, and the head bee-nurse came running up, but this time she was fearfully angry.

"You must mind what you are doing, my good grub," she said. "You are the youngest of them all, and you are the worst for making a noise. Next time I shall tell the queen."

"First listen to me," said the grub, and she told her about the queen's wicked design.

"Good gracious! is that true?" cried the old nurse, and beat her wings in horror. And without hearing a word more, she hurried off to tell the other bees.

"I think I deserve a little honey for what I have done," said the little grub. "But I can now lie down and sleep with a good conscience."

Next evening, when the queen thought that all the bees were in bed, she came to kill the princesses. The grub could hear her talking aloud to herself. But she was quite afraid of the wicked queen, and dared not stir.

"I hope she won't kill the princesses," she thought, and squeezed herself nearer to the door to hear what happened.

The queen looked cautiously round on all sides, and then opened the first of the doors. But at the same moment the bees swarmed out from all directions, seized her by the legs and wings, and dragged her out.

"What is the matter?" she cried. "Are you raising a rebellion?"

"No, your majesty," answered the bees, with great reverence; "but we know that you are intending to kill the princesses, and that you shall not be allowed to do. What would become of us in the autumn after your majesty's death?"

"Let me go!" cried the queen, and tried to get away. "I am queen now anyway, and have the power to do what I like. How do you know that I shall die in the autumn?"

But the bees held her fast, and dragged her outside the hive. There they set her free, but she shook her wings in a passion and said to them,—

"You are disloyal subjects, who are not worth ruling over. I won't stay here an hour longer, but I will go out into the world and build a new nest. Are there any of you who will come with me?"

Some of the old bees, who had been grubs at the same time as the queen, declared that they would follow her. And soon after they flew away.

"Now we have no queen," said the others, "we must take good care of the princesses." And so they crammed them with honey from morning till night;

and they grew, and grabbed, and squabbled, and made more noise each day than the day before.

As for the little grub, no one gave a single thought to her.

One morning the doors of the princesses' chambers flew open, and all ten of them stepped out, beautiful full-grown queen bees. The other bees ran up and gazed at them in admiration.

"How pretty they are!" they said. "It is hard to say which is the most beautiful."

"I am!" one cried.

"You make a mistake," said another, and stabbed her with her sting.

"You are rather conceited," shrieked a third. "I imagine that I am rather prettier than you are."

And immediately they all began calling out at once, and soon after began to fight with one another as hard as ever they could.

The bees would have liked to separate them, but the old head bee-nurse said to them,—

"Let them go on fighting; then we shall see which of them is the strongest, and we will choose her to be our queen. We can't do with more than one."

At this the bees formed round in a ring and looked on at the battle. It lasted a long time, and it was fiercely fought. Wings and legs which had been bitten off were flying about in the air, and after some time eight of the princesses lay dead upon the ground. The two last were still fighting. One of them had lost all her wings, and the other had only four legs left.

"She will be a poor sort of queen whichever of the two we get," said one of the bees. "We should have done better to have kept the old one."

But she might have spared herself the remark, for in the same moment the princesses gave each other such a stab with their stings that they both fell dead as a door-nail.

"That is a pretty business!" called the bees, and ran about among each other in dismay. "Now we have no queen! What shall we do? what shall we do?"

In despair they crawled about the hive, and did not know which way to turn. But the oldest and cleverest sat in a corner and held a council. For a long time they talked this way and that as to what they should decide on doing in their unhappy circumstances. But at last the head bee-nurse got a hearing, and said,—

"I can tell you how you can get out of the difficulty, if you will but follow my advice. I remember that the same misfortune happened to us in this hive a long time ago. I was then a grub myself. I lay in my cell, and distinctly heard what took place. All the princesses had killed one another, and the old queen had gone out into the world: it was just as it is now. But the bees took one of us grubs and laid her in one of the princesses' cells. They fed her every day with the finest and best honey in the whole hive; and when she was full-grown, she was a charming and good queen. I can clearly remember the whole affair, for I thought at the time that they might just as well have taken me. But we may do the same thing again. I propose that we act in the same way."

The bees were delighted, and cried that they would willingly do so, and they ran off at once to fetch a grub.

"Wait a moment," cried the head bee-nurse, "and take me with you. At any rate, I will come and help you. Consider now. It must be one of the youngest grubs, for she must have time to think over her new position. When one has been brought up to be a mere drudge, it is not easy to accustom oneself to wear a crown."

That also seemed to the bees to be wise, and the old one went on,—

"Close by the side of the princesses' cells lies a little grub. She is the youngest of them all. She must have learnt a good deal by hearing the princesses' refined conversation, and I have noticed that she has some character. Besides, it was she who was honourable enough to tell me about the wicked intentions of the old queen. Let us take her."

At once they went in a solemn procession to the six-sided cell where the little grub lay. The head bee-nurse politely knocked at the door, opened it cautiously, and told the grub what the bees had decided. At first she could hardly believe her own ears; but when they had carried her carefully into one of the large, delightful chambers, and brought her as much honey as she could eat, she perceived that it was all in earnest.

"So I am to be queen after all," she said to the head bee-nurse. "You would not believe it, you old growler!"

"I hope that your majesty will forget the rude remarks that I made at the time you lay in the six-sided cell," said the old bee, with a respectful bow.

"I forgive you," said the new-baked princess. "Fetch me some more honey."

A little time after the grub was full grown, and stepped out of her cell as big and as beautiful as the bees could wish. And besides, she knew how to command.

"Away with you!" she said. "We must have more honey for our use in the winter, and you others must perspire more wax. I am thinking of building a new wing to the hive. The new princesses shall live there next year; it is very unsuitable for them to be so near common grubs."

"Heyday!" said the bees to one another. "One would think she had been a queen ever since she lay in the egg."

"No," said the head bee-nurse; "that is not so. But she has had queenly thoughts, and that is the great thing."

The Anemones

"Peeweet! peeweet!" cried the plover, as he flew over the bog in the wood. "My Lady Spring is coming! I can tell it from the feeling in my legs and wings."

When the new grass that lay below in the earth heard that, it pushed up at once and peeped out merrily from among the old yellow grass of last year. For the grass is always in a great hurry.

The anemones in among the trees also heard the plover's cry; but they, on the contrary, would not come up yet on any account.

"You must not believe the plover," they whispered to one another. "He is a gay young spark who is not to be depended upon. He always comes too early, and begins crying out at once. No, we will wait quietly till the starlings and swallows come. They are sensible, steady-going people who know what's what, and don't go sailing with half a wind."

And then the starlings came. They perched on the stumps in front of their summer villa, and looked about them.

"Too early as usual," said Daddy Starling. "Not a green leaf and not a fly to be seen, except an old tough one from last year, which isn't worth opening one's bill for."

Mother Starling said nothing, but she did not seem any more enchanted with the prospect.

"If we had only stayed in our cosy winter home down there beyond the mountains," said Daddy Starling. He was angry at his wife's not answering him, because he was so cold that he thought it might do him good to have a little fun. "But it is your fault, as it was last year. You are always in such a dreadful hurry to come out to the country."

"If I am in a hurry, I know the reason for it," said Mother Starling. "And you ought to be ashamed of yourself if you didn't know it also, since they are your eggs just as much as mine."

"What do you mean?" said Daddy Starling, much insulted. "When have I neglected my family? Perhaps you even want me to sit in the cold and sing to you?"

"Yes, I do," said Mother Starling in the tone he couldn't resist.

He began to pipe at once as well as he knew how. But Mother Starling had no sooner heard the first notes than she gave him a flap with her wings and snapped at him with her beak.

"Oh, please stop it!" she cried bitterly. "It sounds so sad that it makes one quite heartsick. Instead of piping like that, get the anemones to come up. I think it must be time for them. And besides, one always feels warmer when there are others freezing besides oneself."

Now as soon as the anemones had heard the first piping of the starling, they cautiously stuck out their heads from the earth. But they were so tightly wrapped up in green kerchiefs that one could not get a glimpse of them. They looked like green shoots which might turn into anything.

"It is too early," they whispered. "It is a shame of the starling to entice us out. One can't rely on anything in the world nowadays."

Then the swallow came.

"Chee! chee!" he twittered, and shot through the air on his long, tapering wings. "Out with you, you stupid flowers! Don't you see that my Lady Spring has come?"

But the anemones had grown cautious. They only drew their green kerchiefs a little apart and peeped out.

"One swallow does not make a summer," they said. "Where is your wife? You have only come here to see if it is possible to stay here, and you want to take us in. But we are not so stupid. We know very well that if we once catch a bad cold we are done for, for this year at any rate."

MY LADY SPRING

"You are cowards," said the swallow, perching himself on the forest-ranger's weathercock, and peering out over the landscape.

But the anemones waited still and shivered. A few of them who could not control their impatience threw off their kerchiefs in the sun. The cold at night nipped and killed them; and the story of their pitiful death was passed on from flower to flower, and caused a great consternation.

And then—one delightfully mild, still night—my Lady Spring came.

No one knows how she looks, because no one has ever seen her. But all long for her, and thank her and bless her. She goes through the wood and touches the flowers and trees, and at once they burst out. She goes through the cattle-stalls and unties the beasts, and lets them out on to the field. She goes straight into the hearts of men and fills them with gladness. She makes it hard for the best boy to sit still on his form at school, and she is the cause of a terrible number of mistakes in the copy-books.

But she does not do all this at once. Night after night she plies her task, and she comes first to him who longs for her most.

So it happened that on the very night of her coming she went straight to the anemones, who stood in their green kerchiefs and didn't know how to hold out any longer.

And one, two, three! there they stood in their newly-ironed white collars, and looked so fresh and so pretty that the starlings sang their prettiest songs out of sheer joy in them.

"Ah, how sweet it is here!" said the anemones. "How warm the sun is, and how the birds sing! It is a thousand times better than last year."

But they said the same thing every year, so one needn't take any account of it.

There were many others who were quite beside themselves when they saw the anemones had come out. One was a schoolboy who wanted to have his summer holidays at once; and another was the beech tree, who felt exceedingly put out.

"Aren't you coming soon to me, my Lady Spring?" he said. "I am a much more important person than those silly anemones, and I can't really hold in my buds much longer."

"I am coming, I am coming," answered my Lady Spring. "But you must give me a little time."
She went on her way through the wood, and at every step many and many an anemone burst into flower. They stood in crowds round the roots of the birch tree, and bashfully bowed their round heads to the earth.

"Look up," said my Lady Spring, "and rejoice in God's bright sunshine. Your life is short, so you must enjoy it while you have it."

The anemones did as she told them. They stretched and strained, and spread their white petals to all sides, to drink as much sunshine as they could. They pushed their heads against one another, and twined their stalks together, and laughed, and were immensely happy.

"Now I can wait no longer," said the beech, and he burst into leaf.

Leaf after leaf crept forth from its green sheath and waved in the wind. The great tree made a green arch, like a mighty roof over the earth.

"Dear me, is it already evening?" asked the anemones, who noticed that it had grown quite dark.

"No; it is Death," said my Lady Spring. "Now your time is over. It happens to you just as it happens to all that is best on earth. Everything in turn must spring to life, and bloom, and die."

"Die?" cried some little anemones. "Must we die already?"

And some of the big ones grew quite red in the face in their terror and vexation.

"We know what it is," they said. "It is the beech that is the death of us. He steals the sunshine for his own leaves, and does not allow us a single ray. He is a mean, wicked thing."

They stood for some days, grumbling and crying. Then my Lady Spring came for the last time through the wood. She had still the oak trees and some other crusty old fellows to attend to.

"Lie down nicely in the earth and go to sleep," she said to the anemones. "It is of no use to kick against the pricks. Next year I will come back and waken you once more to life."

And some of the anemones did as she told them. But others still stretched their heads into the air, and grew so ugly and stalky that it was horrid to see them.

"Fie for shame!" they cried to the beech leaves. "It is you who are killing us."

But the beech shook his long boughs and let his brown husks drop down to the ground.

"Wait till the autumn, you little simpletons," he said, laughing. "Then you shall see."

The anemones could not understand what he meant. But when they had stretched themselves till they were as tall as they could be, they broke off and withered.

The summer was over, and the farmer had carried his corn home from the field.
The wood was still green, but it was a darker green than before; and in many places red and yellow leaves glowed among the green ones. The sun was tired after his hot work in the summer, and went early to bed.

At night Winter was stealing about among the trees to see if his time was not soon coming. When he found a flower, he gallantly kissed it, saying,—

"What! are you here still? I am charmed to meet you. Please stay where you are. I am a good old man, and would not harm a cat."

But the flower shuddered at his kiss, and the transparent dewdrop that hung from its petal froze to ice at the instant.

Again and again Winter ran through the wood. When he breathed on them, the leaves turned yellow and the earth grew hard.

Even the anemones, who lay below in the earth waiting till my Lady Spring should come back as she had promised, they too felt his breath and shuddered down in their roots.

"Ugh! how cold it is!" they said to one another. "How shall we stand the winter? We shall die for a certainty before it is over."

"Now it's my time," said Winter. "Now I need no longer steal about like a thief in the night. After to-day I shall look everybody in the face, and bite their noses, and make their eyes run with water."

At night he let loose the storm. "Let me see you make a clean sweep," he said. And the storm obeyed his command. He went howling through the wood, and shook the branches till they creaked and cracked. Any that were rotten broke off, and those that held on had to turn and bow this way and that.

"Away with that finery!" howled the storm as he tore off the leaves. "This is not the time to dress yourself up. The snow will soon be coming on to your branches; that will be quite another story."

All the leaves fell in terror to the earth, but the storm would not let them rest. He seized them round the waist and waltzed with them out over the field, high up into the air, and into the wood again, swept them into great heaps, and then scattered them in all directions—just as it pleased him.

Not till morning came did the storm grow weary and lie down to rest.

"Now you shall have peace for a time," he said. "I will take a rest till we have the spring cleaning. Then we can have another turn together—that is, if there are any of you left by then."

And the leaves lay down to rest, and spread themselves like a thick carpet over the whole land.

The anemones felt that it had become pleasantly warm.

"Can it be my Lady Spring already?" they asked each other.

"I haven't got my buds ready," shouted one of them.

"Nor I! Nor I!" cried the others in one voice.

But one of them took courage and peeped out over the earth.

"Good-morning!" cried the withered beech leaves. "It is a little too early, little lady. I hope you will be none the worse for it."

"Isn't it my Lady Spring?" inquired the anemone.

"Not yet," answered the beech leaves. "It is only the green beech leaves that you were so angry with last summer. The green has gone from us, so we have no great finery to boast of now. We have enjoyed our youth and had our fling, I can tell you. And now we lie here and protect all the little flowers in the earth against the winter."

"And meanwhile I stand shivering in all my bare boughs," said the beech peevishly.

The anemones talked it over one to another down below in the earth, and thought it was grand.

"Those grand beech leaves!" they said.

"Mind you remember this next summer when I burst into leaf," said the beech.

"We will! we will!" whispered the anemones.

But that sort of promise is easily made—and easily broken.

The Mist

The sun had just gone down.

The frog was croaking his "good-night," which lasted so long that there seemed no end to it. The bee was creeping into its hive, and little children were crying because they had to go to bed. The flower was closing up its petals and bowing its head; the bird was tucking its bill under its wing; and the stag was laying himself down to rest in the tall, soft grass in the glade of the wood.

From the village church the bells were ringing for sunset, and when that was over the old clerk went home. On his way he had a little chat or two with the people who were out for an evening stroll, or were standing before their gate and smoking a pipe till they bade him good-night and shut the door.

Then it grew quite quiet, and the darkness fell. There was a light in the parson's house, and there was one also in the doctor's. But the farmers' houses were dark, because in summer-time the farmers get up so early that they must go early to bed.

And then the stars began to twinkle, and the moon crept higher and higher up the sky. Down in the village a dog was barking. But it must have been barking in a dream, for there was nothing to bark at.

"Is there anybody there?" asked the mist.

But nobody answered, for nobody was there. So the mist issued forth in her bright, airy robes. She went dancing over the meadows, up and down, to and fro. Then she lay quite still for a moment, and then she took to dancing again. Out over the lake she skipped and deep into the wood, where she threw her long, damp arms round the trunks of the trees.

"Who are you, my friend?" asked the night-violet,[A] who stood there giving forth fragrance just to please herself.

[A] An inconspicuous flower which in Denmark is very fragrant in the evening, the "night-smelling rocket" (Hesperis tristis).

The mist did not answer, but went on dancing.

"I asked you who you were," said the night-violet. "And as you don't answer me, I conclude that you are a rude person."

"I will now conclude you," said the mist. And then she spread herself round the night-violet, so that her petals were dashed with wet.

"Oh, oh!" cried the night-violet. "Keep your fingers to yourself, my friend. I have a feeling as if I had been dipped in the pond. You have no reason for getting so angry just because I asked you who you are."

The mist let go of her again.

"Who am I?" she said. "You could not understand even if I told you."

"Try," said the night-violet.

"I am the dewdrop on the flower, the cloud in the sky, and the mist on the meadow," said the mist.

"I beg your pardon," said the night-violet. "Would you mind saying that again? The dewdrop I know. It settles every morning on my leaves, and I don't think it is at all like you."

"No; but it is I all the same," said the mist mournfully. "But no one knows me. I must live my life under many shapes. One time I am dew, and another time I am rain; and yet another time I babble as a clear, cool streamlet through the wood. But when I dance on the meadows in the evening, men say that it is the marsh-lady brewing."

"It is a strange story," said the night-violet. "Do you mind telling it to me? The night is long, and I sometimes get a little bored by it."

"It is a sad story," answered the mist. "But you may have it and welcome."

But when she was about to lie down the night-violet shook with terror in all her petals.

"Be so kind as to keep at a little distance," she said, "at least till you have properly introduced yourself. I have never cared to be on familiar terms with people I don't know."

So the mist lay down a little way off and began her story:—

"I was born deep down in the earth—far deeper than your roots go. There I and my sisters—for we are a large family, you must understand—came into the world as waves of a hidden spring, pure and clear as crystal; and for a long time we had to stay in our hiding-place. But one day we suddenly leapt from a hillside into the full light of the sun. You can well imagine how delightful it was to come tumbling down through the wood. We hopped over stones and rippled against the bank. Pretty little fishes gambolled amongst us, and the trees bent over so that their beautiful green was reflected in our waters. If a leaf fell, we cradled it and fondled it and carried it out with us into the wide world. Ah, that was delightful! It was indeed the happiest time of my life."

"But when are you going to tell me how you came to turn into mist?" asked the night-violet impatiently. "I know all about the underground spring. When the air is quite still, I can hear it murmur from where I stand."

The mist lifted herself a little and took a turn round the meadow. Then she came back, and went on with her story:—

"It is the worst of this world that one is never contented with what one has. So it was with us. We kept running on and on, till at last we ran into a great lake, where water-lilies rocked on the water and dragon-flies hummed on their great stiff wings. Up on the surface the lake was clear as a mirror. But whether we wished it or not, we had to run right down by the bottom, where it was dark and gruesome. And this I could not endure. I longed for the sunbeams. I knew them so well from the time I used to run in the brook. There they used to peep down through the leaves and pass over me in fleeting gleams. I longed so much to see them again that I stole up to the surface, and lay down in the sunshine all amongst the white water-lilies and their great green leaves. But, ugh! how the sun burnt me there on the lake! It was scarcely bearable. Bitterly did I regret that I had not stopped down below."

"I can't say this part of your story is very amusing," said the night-violet. "Isn't the mist soon coming?"

"Here it is!" said the mist, and dropped down once more on the flower, so that it nearly had the breath squeezed out of it.

"Ough! ough!" shrieked the night-violet. "Upon my word, you are the most ill-natured person I have ever known. Move off, and go on with your story, since it must be so."

"In the evening, when the sun had set, I suddenly became wonderfully light," said the mist. "I don't know how it came about, but I thought I could rise up from the lake and fly; and before I knew anything about it, I was drifting over the water, far away from the dragon-flies and the water-lilies. The evening breeze bore me away. I flew high up into the air, and there I met many of my sisters, who had been just as eager for novelty as myself, and had had the same fate. We drifted across the sky, for, you see, we had become clouds."

"I am not sure I do see," said the night-violet. "The thing sounds incredible."

"But it is true all the same," answered the mist. "And let me tell you what happened then. The wind carried us for a long way through the air. But all at once it would not do so any more, and let us drop. Down we fell on to the earth as a splashing shower of rain. The flowers all shut up in a hurry, and the birds crept under cover—except, of course, the ducks and the geese, for, you know, the wetter it is the more they like it. Yes—and the farmer too! He wanted rain so much for his crops, he stood there hugely delighted, and did not in the least mind getting wet. But otherwise we really did make quite a sensation."

"Oh! so you are the rain as well?" said the night-violet. "I must say you have plenty to do."

"Yes, I'm never idle," said the mist.

"All the same, I have not yet heard how you became mist," said the night-violet. "Only, please don't get into a passion again. You know you promised to tell me without my asking you, and I would sooner hear the whole story over again than shiver once more in your horrid, clammy arms."

The mist lay silent and sobbed for a few moments. Then she went on with her story:—

"After I had fallen on the earth as rain, I sank down into the black soil, and was already congratulating myself on soon getting back to my birthplace, the deep underground spring. There, at any rate, one enjoyed peace and had no cares. But, as I was sinking into the ground, the tree roots sucked me up, and I had to wander about for a whole day in the boughs and leaves. They treated me as a beast of burden, I assure you. All the food that the leaves and flowers needed I had to carry up to them from the roots. It was not till the evening that I managed to get away. When the sun had gone down the flowers and trees all heaved a deep sigh, and I and my sisters flew off in that sigh in the form of bright airy mists. To-night we dance on the meadow. But when the sun rises in the morning we shall turn into those pretty transparent dewdrops which hang from your petals. When you shake us off we shall sink deeper and deeper till we reach the spring we came from—that is, if some root or other does not snap us up on the way. And so the journey goes on. Down the brook, out into the lake, up into the air, down again to the earth—"

"Stop!" said the night-violet. "If I listen to you any more, I shall become quite sea-sick."

Now the frog began to stir. He stretched his legs, and went down to the ditch to take his morning bath. The birds began to twitter in the wood, and the bellow of the stag echoed amongst the trees. It was on the point of dawn, and here came the sun peeping up over the hill.

"Hullo, what is that?" he said. "What a strange sight! One can't see one's hand before one's face. Wind of the morning! up with you, you sluggard, and drive the foul mists away."

The morning wind came over the meadow, and away went the mists. And at the very same moment the first rays of the sun fell right on the night-violet.

"Heyday!" said the flower. "We have got the sun already, so I had better make haste and shut up. Where in the world has the mist gone to?"

"I am still here," said the dewdrop that hung on its stalk.

But the night-violet shook herself peevishly. "You may stuff up children with that nonsense," she said. "As for me, I don't believe a word of your whole story. It is as weak as water."

Then the sun laughed and said, "You are quite right there!"

The Beech And The Oak

It all happened long, long ago. There were no towns then with houses and streets, and church steeples domineering over everything. There were no schools, for there were not many boys, and those that there were learnt from their father to shoot with the bow and arrow, to hunt the stag in his covert, to kill the bear in order to make clothes out of his skin, and to rub two pieces of wood together till they caught fire. When they knew this perfectly, they had finished their education. There were no railways either, and no cultivated fields, no ships on the sea, no books, for there was nobody who could read them.

There was scarcely anything except trees. But trees there were in plenty. They stood everywhere from coast to coast; they saw themselves reflected in all the rivers and lakes, and stretched their mighty boughs up towards heaven. They leaned out over the shore, dipped their boughs in the black fen water, and from the high hills looked out proudly over the land.

They all knew each other, for they belonged to a great family, and were proud of it.

"We are all oak trees," they said. "We own the land, and rule over it."

And they were right. There were only a few human beings there in those days, and those that there were were nothing better than wild animals. The bear, the wolf, and the fox went out hunting, while the stag grazed by the edge of the fen. The field-mouse sat outside his hole and ate acorns, and the beaver built his artistic houses by the river banks.

One day the bear came trudging along and lay down at full breadth under a great oak tree.

"Are you there again, you robber?" said the oak, and shook a lot of withered leaves down over him.

"You should not squander your leaves, my old friend," said the bear, licking his paws. "That is all the shade you can give against the sun."

"If you are not pleased with me, you can go," answered the oak proudly. "I am lord in the land, and whatever way you look you find my brothers and nothing else."

"True," muttered the bear. "That is just what is so sickening. I have been for a little tour abroad, I may tell you, and am just a little bit spoilt. It was in a land down towards the south—there I took a nap under the beech trees. They are tall, slim trees, not crooked old things like you. And their tops are so dense that the sunbeams cannot creep through them. It was a real pleasure there to take a midday nap, I assure you."

"Beech trees?" said the oak inquisitively. "What are they?"

"You might well wish you were half as pretty as a beech tree," said the bear. "But I don't want to chatter any more with you just now. I have had to trot a mile on account of a confounded hunter who struck me on one of my hind legs with an arrow. Now I should like to have a sleep, and perhaps you will be kind enough to leave me at peace, since you cannot give me shade."

The bear stretched himself out and closed his eyes; but he got no sleep that time, for the other trees had heard his story, and they began chattering and talking and rustling their leaves in a way never known in the wood before.

"What on earth can those trees be?" said one of them.

"It is, of course, a mere story; the bear wishes to impose upon us," said the other.

"What kind of trees can they be whose leaves sit so close together that the sunbeams cannot creep between them?" asked a little oak, who was listening to what the big ones were talking about.

But by his side stood an old gnarled tree, who gave the little oak a clout on the head with one of his lowest boughs.
"Hold your tongue," he said, "and don't talk till you have something to talk about. You need none of you believe a word of the bear's nonsense. I am much taller than you, and I can see far out over the wood. But so far as ever I can see, there is nothing but oak trees."

The little oak was shamefaced, and held his tongue; and the other big trees spoke to one another in low whispers, for they had great respect for the old one.

But the bear got up and rubbed his eyes. "Now you have disturbed my midday nap," he growled angrily, "and I declare that I will have my revenge. When I come back I will bring some beech nuts with me, and I vow you will all turn yellow with jealousy when you see how pretty the new trees are."

Then he made off. But the oaks talked the whole day long one to another about the funny trees he had told them about.

"If they come, I will kill them," said the little oak tree, but directly afterwards he got one on the head from the old oak.

"If they come, you shall treat them politely, you young dog," said he. "But they will not come."

But in this the old oak was wrong, for they did come.

Towards autumn the bear came back and lay down under the old oak.

"My friends down there wish me to present their compliments," he said, and he picked some funny things out of his shaggy coat. "Here you may see what I have for you."

"What is it?" asked the oak.

"That is beech," answered the bear—"the beech nuts which I promised you."

Then he trampled them into the ground and prepared to go back.

"It is a pity I cannot stay and see how angry you will be," he growled, "but those confounded human beings have begun to press one so hard. The day before yesterday they killed my wife and one of my brothers, and I must see about finding a place where I can live in peace. There is scarcely a spot left where a self-respecting bear can stay. Good-bye, you old, gnarled oak trees!"

When the bear had shambled off, the trees looked at one another anxiously.

"Let us see what comes of it," said the old oak.

And after this they composed themselves to rest. The winter came and tore all their leaves off them, the snow lay high over the whole land, and every tree stood deep in his own thoughts and dreamt of the spring.

And when the spring came the grass stood green, and the birds began singing where they left off last. The flowers came up in multitudes from the earth, and everything looked fresh and gay.

The oak trees alone stood with leafless boughs.

"It is the most dignified thing to come last!" they said one to another. "The kings of the wood do not come till the whole company is assembled."

But at last they came. All the leaves burst forth from the swollen buds, and the trees looked at one another and complimented one another on their beauty. The little oak had grown ever so much. He was very proud of it, and he thought that he had now the right to join in the conversation.

"Nothing has come yet of the bear's beech trees," he said jeeringly, at the same time glancing anxiously up at the old oak, who used to give him one on the head.

The old oak heard what he said very plainly, and the other trees also; but they said nothing. Not one of them had forgotten what the bear had told them, and every morning when the sun came out they peeped down to look for the beeches. They were really a little uneasy, but they were too proud to talk about it.

And one day the little shoots did at last burst forth from the earth. The sun shone on them, and the rain fell on them, so it was not long before they grew tall.

"Oh, how pretty they are!" said the great oak, and stooped his crooked boughs still more, so that they could get a good view of them.

"You are welcome among us," said the old oak, and graciously inclined his head to them. "You shall be my foster-children, and be treated just as well as my own."

"Thanks," said the little beeches, and they said no more.

But the little oak could not bear the strange trees. "It is dreadful the way you shoot up into the air," he said in vexation. "You are already half as tall as I am. But I beg you to take notice that I am much older, and of good family besides."

The beeches laughed with their little, tiny green leaves, but said nothing.

"Shall I bend my branches a little aside so that the sun can shine better on you?" the old tree asked politely.

"Many thanks," answered the beeches. "We can grow very nicely in the shade."

And the whole summer passed by, and another summer after that, and still more summers. The beeches went on growing, and at last quite overtopped the little oak.

"Keep your leaves to yourself," cried the oak; "you overshadow me, and that is what I can't endure. I must have plenty of sunshine. Take your leaves away or I perish."

The beeches only laughed and went on growing. At last they closed together over the little oak's head, and then he died.

"That was a horrid thing to do," a great oak called out, and shook his boughs in terror.

But the old oak took his foster-children under his protection.

"It serves him right," he said. "He is paid out for his boasting. I say it, though he is my own flesh and blood. But now you must behave yourselves, little beeches, or I will give you a clout on the head."

Years went by, and the beeches went on growing, and they grew till they were tall young trees, which reached up among the branches of the old oak.

"You begin to be rather pushing," the old tree said. "You should try to grow a little broader, and stop this shooting up into the air. Just see where your branches are soaring. Bend them properly, as you see us do. How will you be able to hold out when a regular storm comes? I assure you the wind gives one's head a good shaking. My old boughs have creaked many a time; and what do you think will become of the flimsy finery that you stick up in the air?"

"Every one has his own manner of growth, and we have ours," answered the young beeches. "This is the way it's done where we come from, and we are perhaps as good as you are."

"That is not a polite way of speaking to an old tree with moss on his boughs," said the oak. "I begin to repent that I was so kind to you. If you have a spark of honourable feeling alive in you, be good enough to move your leaves a little to one side. There have been scarcely any buds on my lowest branches this year, you overshadow me so."

"I don't quite understand how that concerns us," answered the beeches. "Every one has quite enough to do to look after himself. If he is equal to his work, and has luck, it turns out well for him; if not, he must be prepared to go to the wall. That is the way of the world."

Then the oak's lowest branch died, and he began to be seriously alarmed.

"You are pretty things," he said, "if this is the way you reward me for my hospitality. When you were little I let you grow at my feet, and sheltered you against the storm. I let the sun shine on you as much as ever he would, and I treated you as if you were my own children. And in return for all this you stifle me."

"Stuff and nonsense!" said the beeches. So they put forth flowers and fruit, and when the fruit was ripe the wind shook the boughs and scattered it round far and wide.

"You are quick people like me," said the wind. "I like you for it, and am glad to do you a good turn."

And the fox rolled on the ground at the foot of the beech trees and got his fur full of the prickly fruits, and ran with them far out into the country. The bear did the same, and grinned into the bargain at the old oak while he lay and rested in the shadow of the beeches. The field-mouse was beside himself with joy over his new food, and thought that beech nuts tasted much nicer than acorns. All around new little beech trees shot up, which grew just as fast as their parents, and looked as green and as happy as if they did not know what an uneasy conscience was.

But the old oak gazed sadly out over the wood. The light-green beech leaves were peeping out everywhere, and the oaks were sighing and bewailing their distress to one another.

"They are taking our strength out of us," they said, and shook as much as the beeches around would let them. "The land is ours no longer."

One bough died after another, and the storm broke them off and cast them on the ground. The old oak had now only a few leaves left at the very top.

"The end is near," he said gravely.

By this time there were many more human beings in the land than there were before, and they made haste to hew down the oaks while there were still some remaining.

"Oak timber is better than beech timber," they said.

"At last we get a little appreciation," said the old oak, "but we have to pay for it with our lives."

Then he said to the beech trees,—

"What was I thinking of when I helped you on in your young days? What an old stupid I was! Before that, we oak trees were lords in the land; and now every year I see my brothers around me perishing in the fight against you. It will soon be all over with me, and not one of my acorns has sprouted under your shade. But before I die I should like to know the name you give to such conduct."

"That will not take long to say, old friend," answered the beeches. "We call it competition, and that is not any discovery of our own. It is competition which rules the world."

"I do not know these foreign words of yours," said the oak. "I call it mean ingratitude." And then he died

The Dragon-Fly and the Water-lily

In among the green bushes and trees ran the brook. Tall, straight-growing rushes stood along its banks, and whispered to the wind. Out in the middle of the water floated the water-lily, with its white flower and its broad green leaves.

Generally it was quite calm on the brook. But when, now and again, it chanced that the wind took a little turn over it, there was a rustle in the rushes, and the water-lily sometimes ducked completely under the waves. Then its leaves were lifted up in the air and stood on their edges, so that the thick green stalks that came up from the very bottom of the stream found that it was all they could do to hold fast.

All day long the larva of the dragon-fly was crawling up and down the water-lily's stalk.

"Dear me, how stupid it must be to be a water-lily!" it said, and peeped up at the flower.

"You chatter as a person of your small mind might be expected to do," answered the water-lily. "It is just the very nicest thing there is."

"I don't understand that," said the larva. "I should like at this moment to tear myself away, and fly about in the air like the big, beautiful dragon-flies."

"Pooh!" said the water-lily. "That would be a funny kind of pleasure. No; to lie still on the water and dream, to bask in the sun, and now and then to be rocked up and down by the waves—there's some sense in that!"

The larva sat thinking for a minute or two.

"I have a longing for something greater," it said at last. "If I had my will, I would be a dragon-fly. I would fly on strong, stiff wings along the stream, kiss your white flower, rest a moment on your leaves, and then fly on."

"You are ambitious," answered the water-lily, "and that is stupid of you. One knows what one has, but one does not know what one may get. May I, by the way, make so bold as to ask you how you would set about becoming a dragon-

fly? You don't look as if that was what you were born for. In any case you will
have to grow a little prettier, you gray, ugly thing."

"Yes, that is the worst part of it," the larva answered sadly. "I don't know
myself how it will come about, but I hope it will come about some time or other.
That is why I crawl about down here and eat all the little creatures I can get
hold of."

"Then you think you can attain to something great by feeding!" the water-lily
said, with a laugh. "That would be a funny way of getting up in the world."

"Yes; but I believe it is the right way for me!" cried the dragon-fly grub
earnestly.

"All day long I go on eating till I get fat and big; and one fine day, as I think,
all my fat will turn into wings with gold on them, and everything else that
belongs to a proper dragon-fly!"

The water-lily shook its clever white head.

"Put away your silly thoughts," it said, "and be content with your lot. You can
knock about undisturbed down here among my leaves, and crawl up and down
the stalk to your heart's desire. You have everything that you need, and no
cares or worries—what more do you want?"

"You are of a low nature," answered the larva, "and therefore you have no
sense of higher things. In spite of what you say, I wish to become a dragon-fly."
And then it crawled right down to the bottom of the water to catch more
creatures and stuff itself still bigger.

"I can't understand these animals," it said to itself. "They knock about from
morning till night, chase one another and eat one another, and are never at
peace. We flowers have more sense. Peacefully and quietly we grow up side by
side, bask in the sunshine, and drink the rain, and take everything as it
comes. And I am the luckiest of them all. Many a time have I been floating
happily out here on the water, while the other flowers there on dry land were
tormented with drought. The flowers' lot is the best; but naturally the stupid
animals can't see it."

When the sun went down the dragon-fly larva was sitting on the stalk, saying nothing, with its legs drawn up under it. It had eaten ever so many little creatures, and was so big that it had a feeling as if it would burst. But all the same it was not altogether happy. It was speculating on what the water-lily had said, and it could hardly get to sleep the whole night long on account of its unquiet thoughts. All this speculating gave it a headache, for it was work which it was not used to. It had a back-ache too, and a stomach-ache. It felt just as though it was going to break in pieces, and die on the spot.

When the sky began to grow gray in the early morning it could hold out no longer.

"I can't make it out," it said in despair. "I am tormented and worried, and I don't know what will be the end of it. Perhaps the water-lily is right, and I shall never be anything else but a poor, miserable larva. But that is a fearful thing to think of. I did so long to become a dragon-fly and fly about in the sun. Oh, my back! my back! I do believe I am dying!"

It had a feeling as if its back was splitting, and it shrieked with pain. At that moment there was a rustle among the rushes on the bank of the stream.

"That's the morning breeze," thought the larva; "I shall at least see the sun when I die." And with great trouble it crawled up one of the leaves of the water-lily, stretched out its legs, and made ready to die.

But when the sun rose, like a red ball, in the east, suddenly it felt a hole in the middle of its back. It had a creepy, tickling feeling, and then a feeling of tightness and oppression. Oh, it was torture without end!

Being bewildered, it closed its eyes; but it still felt as though it were being squeezed and crushed. At last it suddenly noticed that it was free; and when it opened its eyes it was floating through the air on stiff, shining wings, a beautiful dragon-fly. Down on the leaf of the water-lily lay its ugly gray larva case.

"Hurrah!" cried the new dragon-fly. "So I have got my darling wish fulfilled!" and it started off at once through the air at such a rate that you would think it had to fly to the ends of the earth.

"The creature has got its desire at any rate," thought the water-lily. "Let us see if it will be any the happier for it."

Two days later the dragon-fly came flying back, and seated itself on the flower of the water-lily.

"Oh, good-morning," said the water-lily. "Do I see you once more? I thought you had grown too fine to greet your old friends."

"Good-day," said the dragon-fly. "Where shall I lay my eggs?"

"Oh, you are sure to find some place," answered the flower. "Sit down for a bit, and tell me if you are any happier now than when you were crawling up and down my stalk, a little ugly larva."

"Where shall I lay my eggs? Where shall I lay my eggs?" screamed the dragon-fly, and flew humming around from place to place, laid one here and one there, and finally seated itself, tired and weary, on one of the leaves.

"Well?" said the water-lily.

"Oh, it was better in the old days—much better," sighed the dragon-fly. "The sunshine is really delightful, and it is a real pleasure to fly over the water; but I have no time to enjoy it. I have been so terribly busy, I tell you. In the old days I had nothing to think about; now I have to fly about all day long to get my silly eggs disposed of. I haven't a moment free. I have scarcely time to eat."

"Didn't I tell you so?" cried the water-lily in triumph. "Didn't I prophesy that your happiness would be hollow?"

"Good-bye," sighed the dragon-fly. "I have not time to listen to your disagreeable remarks. I must lay some more eggs."

But just as it was about to fly off the starling came.

"What a pretty little dragon-fly!" it said; "it will be a delightful tit-bit for my little ones."

Snap! it killed the dragon-fly with its bill, and flew off with it.

"What a shocking thing!" cried the water-lily, as its leaves shook with terror. "Those animals! those animals! They are funny creatures. I do indeed value my quiet, peaceful life. I harm nobody, and nobody wants to pick a quarrel with me. I am very luck—"

It did not finish what it was saying, for at that instant a boat came gliding close by.
"What a pretty little water-lily!" cried Ellen, who sat in the boat. "I will have it!"

She leant over the gunwale and wrenched off the flower. When she had got home she put it in a glass of water, and there it stood for three days among a whole company of other flowers.

"I can't make it out," it said on the morning of the fourth day. "I have not come off a bit better than that miserable dragon-fly."

"The flowers are now withered," said Ellen, and she threw them out of the window.

So there lay the water-lily with its fine white petals on the dirty ground.

The Dragonfly and the Waterlily"

The Weeds

It was a beautiful, fruitful season. Rain and sunshine came by turns just as it was best for the corn. As soon as ever the farmer began to think that things were rather dry, you might depend upon it that next day it would rain. And when he thought that he had had rain enough, the clouds broke at once, just as if they were under his command.

So the farmer was in a good humour, and he did not grumble as he usually does. He looked pleased and cheerful as he walked over the field with his two boys.

"It will be a splendid harvest this year," he said. "I shall have my barns full, and shall make a pretty penny. And then Jack and Will shall have some new trousers, and I'll let them come with me to market."

"If you don't cut me soon, farmer, I shall sprawl on the ground," said the rye, and she bowed her heavy ear quite down towards the earth.

The farmer could not hear her talking, but he could see what was in her mind, and so he went home to fetch his scythe.

"It is a good thing to be in the service of man," said the rye. "I can be quite sure that all my grain will be well cared for. Most of it will go to the mill: not that that proceeding is so very enjoyable, but in that way it will be made into beautiful new bread, and one must put up with something for the sake of honour. The rest the farmer will save, and sow next year in his field."

At the side of the field, along the hedge, and the bank above the ditch, stood the weeds. There were dense clumps of them—thistle and burdock, poppy and harebell, and dandelion; and all their heads were full of seed. It had been a fruitful year for them also, for the sun shines and the rain falls just as much on the poor weed as on the rich corn.

"No one comes and mows us down and carries us to a barn," said the dandelion, and he shook his head, but very cautiously, so that the seeds should not fall before their time. "But what will become of all our children?"

"It gives me a headache to think about it," said the poppy. "Here I stand with hundreds and hundreds of seeds in my head, and I haven't the faintest idea where I shall drop them."

"Let us ask the rye to advise us," answered the burdock.

And so they asked the rye what they should do.

"When one is well off, one had better not meddle with other people's business," answered the rye. "I will only give you one piece of advice: take care you don't throw your stupid seed on to the field, for then you will have to settle accounts with me."

This advice did not help the wild flowers at all, and the whole day they stood pondering what they should do. When the sun set they shut up their petals and went to sleep; but the whole night through they were dreaming about their seed, and next morning they had found a plan.

The poppy was the first to wake. She cautiously opened some little trap-doors at the top of her head, so that the sun could shine right in on the seeds. Then she called to the morning breeze, who was running and playing along the hedge.

"Little breeze," she said, in friendly tones, "will you do me a service?"

"Yes, indeed," said the breeze. "I shall be glad to have something to do."

"It is the merest trifle," said the poppy. "All I want of you is to give a good shake to my stalk, so that my seeds may fly out of the trap-doors."

"All right," said the breeze.

And the seeds flew out in all directions. The stalk snapped, it is true; but the poppy did not mind about that, for when one has provided for one's children, one has really nothing more to do in the world.

The Farmer and His Boys

"Good-bye," said the breeze, and would have run on farther.

"Wait a moment," said the poppy. "Promise me first that you will not tell the others, else they might get hold of the same idea, and then there would be less room for my seeds."

"I am mute as the grave," answered the breeze, running off.

"Ho! ho!" said the harebell. "Haven't you time to do me a little, tiny service?"

"Well," said the breeze, "what is it?"

"I merely wanted to ask you to give me a little shake," said the harebell. "I have opened some trap-doors in my head, and I should like to have my seed sent a good way off into the world. But you mustn't tell the others, or else they might think of doing the same thing."

"Oh! of course not," said the breeze, laughing. "I shall be as dumb as a stone wall." And then she gave the flower a good shake and went on her way.

"Little breeze, little breeze," called the dandelion, "whither away so fast?"

"Is there anything the matter with you too?" asked the breeze.

"Nothing at all," answered the dandelion. "Only I should like a few words with you."

"Be quick then," said the breeze, "for I am thinking seriously of lying down and having a rest."

"You cannot help seeing," said the dandelion, "what a fix we are in this year to get all our seeds put out in the world; for, of course, one wishes to do what one can for one's children. What is to happen to the harebell and the poppy and the poor burdock I really don't know. But the thistle and I have put our heads together, and we have hit on a plan. Only we must have you to help us."

"That makes four of them," thought the breeze, and could not help laughing out loud.

"What are you laughing at?" asked the dandelion. "I saw you whispering just now to the harebell and poppy; but if you breathe a word to them, I won't tell you anything."

"Why, of course not," said the breeze. "I am mute as a fish. What is it you want?"

"We have set up a pretty little umbrella on the top of our seeds. It is the sweetest little plaything imaginable. If you will only blow a little on me, the seeds will fly into the air and fall down wherever you please. Will you do so?"

"Certainly," said the breeze.

And ush! it went over the thistle and the dandelion and carried all the seeds with it into the cornfield.

The burdock still stood and pondered. Its head was rather thick, and that was why it waited so long. But in the evening a hare leapt over the hedge.

"Hide me! Save me!" he cried. "The farmer's dog Trusty is after me."

"You can creep behind the hedge," said the burdock, "then I will hide you."

"You don't look to me much good for that job," said the hare, "but in time of need one must help oneself as one can." And so he got in safety behind the hedge.

"Now you may repay me by taking some of my seeds with you over into the cornfield," said the burdock; and it broke off some of its many heads and fixed them on the hare.

A little later Trusty came trotting up to the hedge.

"Here's the dog," whispered the burdock, and with one spring the hare leapt over the hedge and into the rye.

"Haven't you seen the hare, burdock?" asked Trusty. "I see I have got too old
to go hunting. I am quite blind in one eye, and I have completely lost my scent."

"Yes, I have seen him," answered the burdock; "and if you will do me a
service, I will show you where he is."

Trusty agreed, and the burdock fastened some heads on his back, and said to
him,—

"If you will only rub yourself against the stile there in the cornfield, my seeds
will fall off. But you must not look for the hare there, for a little while ago I saw
him run into the wood."

Trusty dropped the burs on the field and trotted to the wood.

"Well, I've got my seeds put out in the world all right," said the burdock, and
laughed as if much pleased with itself; "but it is impossible to say what will
become of the thistle and the dandelion, and the harebell and the poppy."

Spring had come round once more, and the rye stood high already.

"We are pretty well off on the whole," said the rye plants. "Here we stand in a
great company, and not one of us but belongs to our own noble family. And we
don't get in each other's way in the very least. It is a grand thing to be in the
service of man."

But one fine day a crowd of little poppies, and thistles and dandelions, and
burdocks and harebells poked up their heads above ground, all amongst the
flourishing rye.

"What does this mean?" asked the rye. "Where in the world are you sprung
from?"

And the poppy looked at the harebell and asked, "Where do you come from?"

And the thistle looked at the burdock and asked, "Where in the world have
you come from?"

They were all equally astonished, and it was an hour before they had explained. But the rye was the angriest, and when she had heard all about Trusty and the hare and the breeze she grew quite wild.

"Thank heaven, the farmer shot the hare last autumn," she said; "and Trusty, fortunately, is also dead, the old scamp. So I am at peace, as far as they are concerned. But how dare the breeze promise to drop the seeds of the weeds in the farmer's cornfield?"

"Don't be in such a passion, you green rye," said the breeze, who had been lying behind the hedge and hearing everything. "I ask no one's permission, but do as I like; and now I'm going to make you bow to me."

Then she passed over the young rye, and the thin blades swayed backwards and forwards.

"You see," she said, "the farmer attends to his rye, because that is his business. But the rain and the sun and I—we attend to all of you without respect of persons. To our eyes the poor weed is just as pretty as the rich corn."

The farmer now came out to look at his rye, and when he saw the weeds in the cornfield he scratched his head with vexation and began to growl.

"It's that scurvy wind that's done this," he said to Jack and Will, as they stood by his side with their hands in the pockets of their new trousers.

But the breeze flew towards them and knocked all their caps off their heads, and rolled them far away to the road. The farmer and the two boys ran after them, but the wind ran faster than they did.

It finished up by rolling the caps into the village pond, and the farmer and the boys had to stand a long time fishing for them before they got them out.

PREPARING for FLIGHT

The Sparrow

The swallow was in a bad temper. He sat on the roof close by the starlings' box and drooped his bill.

"There is not a fly left to chase," he whined piteously. "They are all gone, and I am so hungry—so hungry!"

"This morning I could not get a single worm," said the starling, and shook his head wisely.

The stork came strutting along, and stood on one leg in the ploughed field just outside the garden, and looked most melancholy.

"I suppose none of you have seen a frog?" he asked. "There isn't one down in the marsh, and I have not had any breakfast to-day."

Then the thrush flew up and perched on the roof of the starlings' box.

"How crestfallen you all are," he said. "What is the matter with you?"

"Ah," answered the starling, "there's nothing else the matter, only the leaves are beginning to fall off the trees, and the butterflies and flies and worms are all eaten up."

"Yes, that is bad for you," said the thrush.

"Well, isn't it just as bad for you, you conceited creature?" said the swallow.

But the thrush piped gaily and shook his head.

"Not quite," he said. "I have always the fir trees, which don't lose their leaves; and I can live very many weeks yet on all the delicious berries in the wood."

"Let us stop squabbling," said the stork. "We had better consider together what we are to do."

"We can soon agree about that," answered the starling, "for we have no choice. We must travel. All my little ones can fly quite well now; we have been drilling every morning down in the meadow. I have already warned them that we shall be starting off one of these days."

The other birds thought this very sensible—all except the thrush, who thought there was no hurry. So they agreed to collect next day down in the meadow, and hold a grand review of the party that was to travel.

They flew off, each to his own quarters; but up under the roof sat the sparrow, who had heard all they had been saying.

"Ah, if only I could travel with them!" he said to himself. "I should so like to see foreign lands. My neighbour the swallow has told me how delightful it is. Such a lot of flies and cherries and corn, and it's so delightfully warm. But no one asks me to fly with him. I am only a poor sparrow, and the others are birds of wealth and position."

He sat thinking it all over for a long time, and the more he thought the sadder he became. When the swallow came home in the evening, the sparrow asked if he could not get him leave to travel with them.

"You? You want to go with us?" asked the swallow, laughing at him scornfully. "You would soon be sick of it. It means flying, flying over land and sea, over hill and dale. Many and many a mile we fly in one journey without a rest. How do you imagine your short wings are going to support you so long as that?"

"Oh, but I should so like to go with you," the sparrow pleaded. "Couldn't you get leave for me to fly with the rest? I have such a longing for it. I must go with you."

"I believe you are mad," said the swallow. "You forget who you are."

"Oh no," said the sparrow.

But the swallow took it upon him to instruct him about his position in society.

"Don't you see," he said, "the rich merchant who lived here in the country during the summer has now moved into town, and the baron who lives on Tower Island has done the same? The painter who was staying out here is also by this time in Copenhagen; and they won't come out here again till next spring. We birds of high station act in the same way. As soon as ever we smell winter, we make our way to lands where life is more enjoyable—to the warm south. But you poor wretches must of course stay at home and suffer. That is how things are arranged in this world. It is just the same with day labourers, and cottagers, and other poor folks."

The sparrow said nothing to this long speech; but when the swallow dropped asleep in his nest, he lay awake and wept over his hard fate. He had still not quite given up hope of going with them all the same.

Next day the birds came flying from all directions, and settled down in the meadow. There were starlings and storks and swallows, besides many little singing-birds. But neither the cuckoo nor the nightingale was there, for they had left long ago. "Fall in!" commanded an old stork. He had been ten times in Egypt, and was therefore reckoned the wisest of them all.

All the birds lined up, and then the oldest and most experienced went round and saw if they had their travelling equipment in order. All those who had their wings rumpled, or had lost some of their tail-feathers, or did not look strong and well, were dismissed or chased away. If they did not obey commands at once, they were beaten to death without mercy.

You may be sure there was a great disturbance when they discovered the sparrow, who had flown up without being noticed, and had planted himself in the ranks with the others.

"A creature like that!" the starling called out. "He wants to go too!"

"Such a pair of wings!" said the swallow. "He thinks that with them he can fly to Italy!"

And all the birds of passage began to scream at once and laugh at the poor sparrow, who sat quite terrified in the midst of them.

"I know quite well," he said humbly, "that I am only a poor little sparrow. But I should so like to see the warm, pleasant lands you are going to. Try to take me with you. I will use my wings as well as ever I can. I implore you to let me come!"

"He has some cheek, hasn't he?" said the old stork. "But he shall be allowed to keep his miserable life. Chase him away at once, and then let us be off!"

So the birds chased the sparrow away, and he hid his miserable self under the eaves.

When the review was over, the birds of passage began to make off. Company after company, they flew away through the air, whilst the sparrow peered out from under the eaves and gazed sadly after them.

"Now they have all gone," he said. "No one but me is left behind."

"Me too!" screamed the crow.

"And me," said the chaffinch.

"And me too, if you please," peeped the tomtit.

"Yes," said the sparrow, "that is how it is. It is just as the swallow says—all we poor birds must stay here and suffer."

The winter had come. Over all the fields lay the snow, and there was ice on the water. All the leaves lay dead and shrivelled on the ground; and there were no flowers, except here and there a poor frozen daisy, which stood gleaming white among the yellow grass.

And the flies and the gnats, and the butterflies and the cockchafers were dead. The snake lay torpid, and so did the lizard. The frog had gone into his winter quarters at the bottom of the pond, sitting deep in the mud, with only his nose sticking up into the air. And that was how he intended to sit the whole winter through.

The birds who had remained behind had not, after all, such a very bad time of it. The crows held great gatherings every evening in the wood, and screamed and chattered so loudly one could hear them ever so far away. The chaffinch and the tomtit hopped about cheerfully enough in the bushes, and picked up what they could find. The sparrow alone was always out of sorts. He sat on the ridge of the roof and hunched himself up, but the whole time he was thinking about the birds of passage.

"They are there by this time," he said to himself. "Here we have ice and snow; but down south, in the pleasant, warm countries, they have endless summer. Here I have a job to find even some dry bread; but there they have more than they can manage to eat. Ah, if one only had gone with them!"

"Come down and join us," called the chaffinch and the tomtit.

But the sparrow shook his head, and remained sitting on the ridge of the roof.

"I am consumed with longing, I can't endure it!" he screamed, and he took a long flight to cool his blood.

But it was of no use. Wherever he came, it seemed to him that everything was so wretched and bare.

Out in the field the lark was flying up to the sky and singing its trills.

"Good-morning, sparrow," it twittered. "I am glad to see that you have not gone away. I am also staying on, as long as I can stand it. It is so delightful at home here, even in winter. Only see how the trees have decked themselves out with hoarfrost, how the ice glistens, and how gleaming white the snow is!"

"It is miserable," said the sparrow. "Poverty and want everywhere."

But the lark did not hear a word of what he said; he flew on his way, singing joyously.

"Craw!" screamed the black jackdaws. "The winter is not so bad after all." And then they walked proudly round the field and looked about on all sides, for they knew that they cut a fine figure against the white snow.

"The winter is really quite peaceful," said the field-mouse, as he stuck his nose out of his hole. "If only it doesn't stay too long, the food will last. I filled my pantry well last summer, and as long as one has food one can always keep warm."
The sparrow heard it all, but it did not do him a bit of good.

"They seem to be contented enough with their lot," he said to himself, "and I suppose it is all right for them. But this miserable life of mine does not satisfy me!"

So he flew home in the sulks, and settled himself again on the ridge of the roof.

"Oh, I know what I will do," he cried suddenly. "I will creep into the swallow's nest and sleep there to-night, then I can dream that I am a swallow."

And he did so, and dreamt all night that he was flying over hill and dale, over land and sea, all the way to Italy. He thought he was so light, so free, and his wings carried him as straight as an arrow through the air. It was the most delightful dream he had ever had.

After this he crept every evening into the swallow's nest, and lay there till ever so late in the morning. When he came out, he sat crunched up on the ridge of the roof or in the bare lime tree. If the gardener's wife had not thrown out some crumbs to him now and then, he would certainly have starved to death. For he didn't care a rap about anything; he merely longed for the evening to come, so that he could dream again. Every evening he dreamt the same thing, but he never grew tired of it.

"This is nearly as good as actually going with them," he thought. "If only I could dream in the daytime in the same way."

But in time his head got quite muddled, and he paid no attention to anything.

Little by little the winter was slipping away, and now it was gone altogether. The days grew longer, and there was more warmth in the sunshine.

"What! are you still here?" said the sun. And he stared so hard at the snow that at last it grew quite bashful, and melted away and sank into the earth.

"Wait a moment," said the cloud to the sun; "we must have a thorough cleaning before your turn comes."

So it fell like a sousing rain on the earth, washing the leaves of the trees and bushes, and collecting into quite a little lake on the ice.

"Now I am coming! now I am coming!" said the real lake, which lay below, under the ice.

It heaved its breast, and with a great sigh the roof of ice burst, and all the little scales began hopping and dancing like boys who have escaped from school.

Then the sun broke out from the cloud, and a thousand little green shoots peeped up from the earth.

"Lend me your wings," said the winter to the storm; "I must be off."

And away it flew to the cold lands right away in the north, where there is winter always.

At last a message came from my Lady Spring that now they might expect her any day.

The only person who saw nothing of what was going on was the sparrow. The whole day he lay there in the swallow's nest, only flying out for a quarter of an hour to take a little bit of food. He hadn't the least idea that it was now going to be summer again. He had grown quite silly, and imagined that he was the swallow.

But one day the swallow came back.

"Chee! chee!" he peeped; "is everything in order to receive us?"

This is what he wished first of all to see about, and so he flew all day long over cornfield and meadow.

"There are not many gnats here yet, but they may still come," he said in the evening when he came home.

Then he peeped into the starlings' box to say "How-do" to his neighbours; but it chanced that at the moment there was no one at home, so he got ready to go to bed.
But when he was going to creep into his nest he noticed there was somebody there already.

"What's this?" he said. "Who has taken the liberty to borrow my nest?"

"It is not yours," said the sparrow, who was lying there. "I am the swallow, and I have just come home from Africa. You may take my word for it, it was delightful there. I have heaps of things to tell you."

The swallow sat for a moment quite speechless. Then he screamed out in a furious passion,—

"You may take my word for it, I shall have something to say to you, you wretched sparrow! I might have guessed it was you who had the impudence to steal my nest. I noticed you were a little cracked even last year. Now, look sharp and come out of that. At once, I say!"

But it was no good the swallow's screaming and threatening. The sparrow was quite sure that he was in the right. He went on telling the swallow how he had just come home from Africa, and was so tired he really must have a quiet time to sleep.

"I will have my revenge," said the swallow as he flew away.

And there in the nest the sparrow lay asleep, dreaming of the warm, delightful land with all the gnats and flies and cherries.

He was still lying fast asleep when, in the middle of the night, the swallow came back. He had filled his broad bill with mud, and quite quietly began to wall up the hole into the nest. To and fro he flew the whole night long, and by the time the sun rose the hole was quite closed up.

"Now he's happy," thought the swallow, as he began to build himself a new nest.

Three days later the swallow and the starling met in the meadow. They said, "How do you do?" and told each other all they had gone through since they last saw one another.

"The most remarkable thing comes last," said the swallow. "Just fancy! When I came home I found the sparrow had taken my nest, and I could not get him to come out."

"Well, I never!" cried the starling. "What on earth did you do to him?"

"Come and see," answered the swallow.

They both flew off to the nest, and the swallow told him how he had taken his revenge. Then they pecked a hole with their bills, and out fell the poor sparrow to the ground quite dead.

"It serves him right," said the swallow.

And the starling nodded, for he thought so too.

But the chaffinch and the tomtit stood below on the ground and gazed at the dead bird.

"Poor sparrow!" said the chaffinch. "I am sorry for him."

"He couldn't expect a better fate," said the tomtit. "He was ambitious; and that is what one has no right to be when one is only a sparrow."